Little Red Riding Hood

by Jackie Walter and Bill Bolton

FRANKLIN WATTS
LONDON•SYDNEY

Once upon a time, there was a girl called Little Red Riding Hood.

She lived with her mother

in a little house near the forest.

One day, Mother said,

"Your grandmother is ill.

You may take some cakes to her.

Stay on the path through the forest.

Remember, don't talk to any strangers."

Little Red Riding Hood walked
through the forest. But when she saw
a beautiful butterfly, she followed it.
She forgot all about what Mother
had told her.

The Big Bad Wolf was watching her
from behind a bush.
"I would like to eat her," he said
to himself.

The Big Bad Wolf crept up to
Little Red Riding Hood.
"Where are you going?" he asked.
"I'm going to Grandmother's house
to take her some cakes,"
said Little Red Riding Hood.

Then Little Red Riding Hood

remembered what Mother had said.

She ran back to the path.

The wolf smiled to himself.

He knew a shortcut through the forest

to Grandmother's house.

Soon, the Big Bad Wolf arrived

at Grandmother's house.

He knocked on the door.

"Who is it?" called Grandmother.

"It's me, Grandmother," called the wolf

in a small voice. "I have cakes for you."

"Come in, dear," called Grandmother.

"I'm in bed."

The Big Bad Wolf hurried
into Grandmother's house
and locked her in the wardrobe.

He put on one of Grandmother's bonnets
and a nightgown, and got into her bed.
"Now, I'll wait for the girl," he said.

Soon, there was a knock at the door.

"It's me, Grandmother!"

called Little Red Riding Hood.

"I have cakes for you."

"Come in, dear!" called the wolf

in a small voice.

Little Red Riding Hood went into

Grandmother's bedroom.

"Why, Grandmother, what big eyes you have!" said Little Red Riding Hood. "All the better to see you with," replied the wolf.

"And what big ears you have!" said Little Red Riding Hood. "All the better to hear you with!" replied the wolf.

"And what big teeth you have,"
said Little Red Riding Hood.
"All the better to EAT you with!"
growled the wolf. He leaped out of bed
to gobble up Little Red Riding Hood.

Just then, a woodcutter burst in through the door. He had seen the wolf in the forest and followed Little Red Riding Hood to make sure she was safe. The woodcutter struck the wolf with his axe.

Then he let Grandmother out of
the wardrobe.

"Thank you!" said Grandmother.

She gave Little Red Riding Hood a hug.

"I will never talk to strangers again,"
said Little Red Riding Hood.

Story order

Look at these 5 pictures and captions.
Put the pictures in the right order
to retell the story.

1

Little Red Riding Hood talked to
the Big Bad Wolf.

2

Little Red Riding Hood walked
through the forest.

3

The woodcutter stopped the Big Bad Wolf.

4

The Big Bad Wolf got into bed.

5

The wolf tried to eat Little Red Riding Hood.

Guide for Independent Reading

This series is designed to provide an opportunity for your child to read on their own. These notes are written for you to help your child choose a book and to read it independently.

In school, your child's teacher will often be using reading books which have been banded to support the process of learning to read. Use the book band colour your child is reading in school to help you make a good choice. *Little Red Riding Hood* is a good choice for children reading at Turquoise Band in their classroom to read independently. The aim of independent reading is to read this book with ease, so that your child enjoys the story and relates it to their own experiences.

About the book

Little Red Riding Hood sets out through the forest to take her grandmother some cakes. But danger lurks in the trees, and the girl is being watched by the Big Bad Wolf ...

Before reading

Help your child to learn how to make good choices by asking: "Why did you choose this book? Why do you think you will enjoy it?" Look at the cover together and ask: "What do you think the story will be about?" Ask your child to think of what they already know about the story context. Then ask your child to read the title aloud.

Ask: "Why do you think the little girl is called Little Red Riding Hood?" Remind your child that they can sound out a word in syllable chunks if they get stuck.

Decide together whether your child will read the story independently or read it aloud to you.

During reading

Remind your child of what they know and what they can do
independently. If reading aloud, support your child if they hesitate or
ask for help by telling the word. If reading to themselves, remind your
child that they can come and ask for your help if stuck.

After reading

Support comprehension by asking your child to tell you about the
story. Use the story order puzzle to encourage your child to retell the
story in the right sequence, in their own words. The correct sequence
can be found on the next page.

Help your child think about the messages in the book that go beyond
the story and ask: "Why do you think Little Red Riding Hood forgot
her mother's warning?"

Give your child a chance to respond to the story: "Did you have
a favourite part? Who was your favourite character?"

Extending learning

Help your child understand the story structure by using the same
sentence patterning and adding different elements. "Let's make up
a new story about Little Red Riding Hood. Where might she be going
this time? What might she do differently?"

In the classroom, your child's teacher may be teaching use of
punctuation marks. Ask your child to identify some question marks
and exclamation marks in the story and then ask them to practise
reading each of the whole sentences with appropriate expression.

Franklin Watts
First published in Great Britain in 2021
by The Watts Publishing Group

Copyright © The Watts Publishing Group 2021

Series Editors: Jackie Hamley and Melanie Palmer
Series Advisors: Dr Sue Bodman and Glen Franklin
Series Designers: Peter Scoulding and Cathryn Gilbert

A CIP catalogue record for this book is
available from the British Library.

ISBN 978 1 4451 7708 3 (hbk)
ISBN 978 1 4451 7710 6 (pbk)
ISBN 978 1 4451 7709 0 (library ebook)
ISBN 078 1 4451 8148 6 (ebook)

Printed in China

Franklin Watts
An imprint of
Hachette Children's Group
Part of The Watts Publishing Group
Carmelite House
50 Victoria Embankment
London EC4Y 0DZ

An Hachette UK Company
www.hachette.co.uk

www.franklinwatts.co.uk

FSC
www.fsc.org
MIX
Paper from
responsible sources
FSC® C104740

Answer to Story order: 2, 1, 4, 5, 3